My Apologies to Tanya Grace

Cat Voleur

The characters and events in this book are fictitious. Any similarity to real persons, living or dead, is coincidental and not intended by the author.

Originally published in Australia by Slashic Horror Press in 2024.

ISBN-13: 978-0-9756380-4-0

Cover design by Christy Aldridge at Grim Poppy Designs

Interior design by Cat Voleur

Edited by David-Jack Fletcher

Other Titles by Cat Voleur

Revenge Arc

Puppet Shark: The Novelization

Kill Your Darlings

The Desert Island Game

To all those who have ever felt haunted.

This one's for you.

Prologue

She watches me while I write this.

Her slender form rests atop my dresser, nestled between half-unpacked boxes of clothing. One knee is folded up to her chest, her chin resting on it as her pale, bruised arms hug the tucked limb close to her body. Her other leg dangles, silent, swinging back and forth.

Everything about her now is as casual and effortless as I remember her being in life.

Everything but her eyes.

They are pools of blue ice that seem to stare straight into my soul. They are daring me to lie, as if the guilt I feel is not already enough in which to drown. They bore into me, and I can tell my ghost is curious.

It isn't that she wants to hear my side of things. We both know it's too late for that.

I believe she wants to see how I'll end the story. Will I concoct something to ease the pain of what transpired? Why not? I've lied before. Lies of omission have been chipping away at me for years, to the point that even I am unsure of what remains.

This is my book, my project. I could tell it how I want. In my own story, do I not deserve to be the heroine?

She doesn't believe I do. I don't blame her. Whether she understands this or not, I have no desire to fabricate a cleaner version of what happened. I, like her, cannot bear the thought of shining on page where I had been so lackluster in life.

In a better world, she would be the one writing this. She should have had a chance to tell all, before the light within her was extinguished. I'm not sure anyone deserves the injustice of having an outsider pen their tale for them. She would have told it better than I can—and not just because she lived it. She had a way with words. I remember she used to write poetry in school. Nonfiction, and hauntingly beautiful.

They were the sort of words that could stick with you.

You'd glimpse a line or two in a notebook, and you would carry those words with you for life. They resonated. *She* resonated.

Maybe I envied her for the way she wrote. Maybe I loved her for it. Maybe there's a reason, aside from the part I played in her demise, that I can't bear the thought of letting her go. She was a near stranger to me, and yet I cannot stand the thought of what she went through. Believe me when I say I can withstand much.

I ache over my survival, is what I mean to say.

Yet I survived. For that reason, I must carry forward and lay it out, despite my doubts that the story is not my own. As a part of my punishment, she will watch me as I go.

So here I go.

My name is Mallory Brennan.

It is so late into Saturday that it reads "Sun" on the calendar of my phone.

I am being haunted by a girl whom I could have saved.

These are facts.

I was scared then. I am petrified now.

These are excuses.

Yet I know this is what it will take to let my ghost retire at long last.

I should get this last part out now, before I begin, so it is not so hard to admit later on.

I am not the heroine of this piece. I'm only the survivor. I know I am haunted for a reason.

For her sake, and my own sanity, I will do what I have not done for a very long time. I will try to be honest. Uncensored. Bad thoughts and all.

She is smirking now.

Either she doesn't believe me, or she thinks I am stalling. I have stalled for long enough.

With the utmost regret, and sympathies in mind, I pen my apologies to Tanya Grace.

Monday (Morning)

I WAS ALREADY IN a weird place when this whole mess began. Leyton is a town for weirdness. Seedy things happen just under the suburban surface that wants so badly to be picturesque, and can never hit the mark. There's a private school. A gym. A Fine Art Museum. Children raised here grow up with the horror stories of what their parents went through, and declarations of how this will be a better time and place for them. It won't be. It never is. The quality of these prestigious developments is lowered by the rotting foundation on which they sit.

I had already clawed my way out once.

It had taken a partial scholarship to college, and a good payout from my father's life insurance policy to see me out of state. I had sworn to myself that I would never step foot in this god forsaken town again. That proved, like so many other things, to be just another lie.

Last Monday was my first official day back.

Before noon I was worn out on my own forced optimism.

My expectations for the town itself were low. My expectations for myself were both high enough to compensate, and impossible to meet.

I had this grand, idyllic vision in my head of what my life was to be in the coming year. I had not taken a gap year between high school and college, but I had the time now, and a little money saved, and was ready to pour myself into my writing for the next twelve months. I'd been dreaming of that my whole last semester, and the idea was so vivid.

I was in love with the idea of a morning writing routine. Waking up, making coffee, writing until noon, and knowing that all other obligations would have to wait until my chapter was done. If I found myself in the zone, they could wait altogether. My book would be my top priority for the whole year, the one thing I cared about. Even if I had to care about it here.

Eric had apologized profusely for the fact that, even though we had selected the apartment together to be closer to his internship, I'd be staying there alone for the first few weeks until his lease was up. I was secretly pleased that I'd have a month to settle into my new fantasy life as an author before I had to share the apartment, and my time.

It was apparent from day one that things were not going to go as planned.

I woke up with a stiff neck and shoulders from sleeping on just the mattress part of the futon. The coffee maker wasn't set up, and I hadn't bought any groceries yet. This meant I had no grounds, no filters. The only thing in place for my routine was my tablet. Like everything else in the new apartment, it was not connected to the internet.

After a quick shower that broke my "coffee and writing first" resolution, I had to dig through several boxes to find anything resembling clean clothes. This turned out to be a fresh T-shirt and the same jeans I'd made the drive in the day before.

My false good humor about my situation had tired me out before I had even found a coffee shop.

The town had been changing in my absence.

Gone were my all comforting corporate establishments, and I settled for the first place I saw: The Northern Grind.

I hated it from the moment I first entered.

The little shop was trying too hard to be casual. The lights were too low, the tables too high. There was a gaggle of college students vaping at one end of the bar, next to noisy coffee grinders that could not be drowned out by the guitars blaring from the speakers. I reminded myself that I would not need to be there often. The visit was simply the means to an end that day, and not a permanent fixture.

I ordered my first cup, black, and I took a seat at a table facing away from the small crowd. I didn't like to think that a month ago, I had been a college kid myself, and probably just as annoying.

I assured myself it would stop annoying me, and that all would feel better while I was writing, but the morning only continued to spiral out from there. I made the mistake of checking my email before I got to work on a fresh document.

There was a message from Patti.

She had been my boss, and my only conduit into the world of freelancing. She owned the New Age Blog vaguely called *The*

Collective that had helped support me all throughout my higher education. While it had felt strange sitting behind a screen and shilling the idea of connecting to nature, it had paid surprisingly well. More importantly, there had been a flexible schedule. I could work more and save more when my homework load was light, but no one had cared if I disappeared for weeks at a time.

The environment had been so laid back in fact, that I had debated over whether or not to bother turning in a letter of resignation. I had done so more out of gratitude than necessity, and at last, the reply had come.

My Darling Mallory,

We will all miss your words and energy. Rest assured, my child, that you are free to return to us at any time, for we shall never again see your like.

Patti and The Collective Team.

It was short and flowery, a style I associated with the strange, infrequent communications with my employer.

Former employer.

Resentment washed over me for the job that I had never felt before. Resentment for her, too.

She'd been good to me, this woman that I had never met. She preached love and kindness and only ever gave good feedback on the column I ghostwrote for her website. I knew she intended this invitation to be kind, as she intended everything, but it felt like a curse.

The idea that I'd return to writing for *The Collective* was one I had not ever considered. It was just my college job. If I had to go back, it would mean that I'd done something terribly wrong, that I'd failed, that I wasn't good enough.

I didn't want to work there forever, picking up enough columns to make full time. I didn't want anonymous spirituality posts to be the extent of my career. I wouldn't have needed to finish my expensive education for that. Plus, it fell far short of my dream to see my name on a book.

With that book in mind, and spite fueling me, I opened up a word document. With determination I typed 'Chapter 1' at the top of the page.

It sat there, alone, while I stared it down for a long time.

I'm not insane.

At least, I wasn't this time last week.

I knew I was not going to just type out a novel on my first try. I know that's not how it works. I had just never been one for outlines. I like messy, rough drafts that could be excavated later—polished and transformed.

I'd been planning scenes for months, considering their roles in the vague webbing of plot that was forming on the back-burner of my brain. I was well-acquainted with the characters. The rainy terrace where the story starts had been so vivid, even just the night before. Yet it seemed my imaginary friends and playground were both absent that day.

My mind began to wander when the words did not immediately come.

I thought about how distracting the music was, and who had picked it. I wondered if I was too old to be hanging out there. Then I worried I was too young to be thinking that way. I contemplated how it might be silly to be starting a manuscript when I didn't even have the apartment set up. A routine wasn't worth as much as a good night's sleep, after all, and the last thing I wanted was another night on the futon cushion. Despite my best efforts, Patti's words slipped into my mind as well. "*You can return to us at any time.*"

This is where my world was. These were the sort of mundane problems I was dealing with.

Professional insecurities, moving anxieties, the way my coffee had dwindled and would need replaced. I stood first, and stretched, with the intention to get a refill.

When I turned back to the counter, she was there.

I saw the braid first, and everything in the room shifted.

The linoleum was turned to green, crunchy carpet. There was no counter between us, and she was standing in front of a wall of shelves. It still smelled and sounded like a coffee shop, but it was just the two of us, and we were in our old classroom.

Her name tag read 'Tammen' but I knew that wasn't right.

She was wearing ripped jeans that pooled over her red Chuck Taylors, faded with time and covered in ink from countless doodles. Her T-shirt was at least two sizes too large, and declared her a member of the school's German Club. Her platinum blonde hair fell down to just below her shoulders, except on the right side where part of it was pulled into a small braid, and tucked neatly behind her ear. She was handing out some sort of flyer, when her blue eyes locked on mine.

The illusion was broken, the glass shattered.

I must have looked foolish standing there, gawking at her, but her gaze didn't fall on me for more than a moment. It was just long enough to confirm that she was truly there, even if everything else in the vision had been my fragmented memories of her.

She was serving coffee behind the counter of the same pretentious place I had stumbled into that morning. She was wearing a baggy gray sweater under the black apron, and her name tag clearly read 'Tanya.'

It was a name I hadn't thought about in years.

Tanya Grace.

When she sat the cup of coffee on the counter, I could see the purple bruise on her wrist where the sleeves of her sweater were folded back.

I'd tie you down if I could.

The voice came to mind, unbidden, out of nowhere. It made my blood run cold, but it wasn't the worst of it.

What made me truly sick was the flash of gold from her ring.

I couldn't see anything after that. My vision was tunneling and I made a rush for the door, worried I'd faint. My purse, tablet, and sanity were left at the table for anyone to pick over while I stood outside and tried to force air into my lungs.

It took a while for breathing to feel okay again. It took longer for my stomach to settle, the bitter coffee in it roiling.

When I came back in, my things were still at the table, but Tanya was nowhere to be seen.

Monday (Afternoon)

THE THING ABOUT REPRESSION is that you don't know you're doing it. Or hell, maybe I was just exceptionally good at lying to myself. I like to think I knew, at one point, but over time I got gradually better and better at pretending to be okay. Then I learned to live with the lie, and I got used to the false sense of normalcy that I'd been chasing.

That's the only explanation I have as to why Monday was the way that it was after my meeting with Tanya.

I didn't remember all at once when I saw her, but the feeling of the encounter hit me like a truck. It's hard to describe the rest of it, because I don't remember it vividly. I was maneuvering on autopilot for the rest of that afternoon and into the early evening.

All I have to say about it, until the phone call, was that I felt heavy.

I don't recall collecting my things or leaving the coffee shop. I don't remember going through the boxes in my apartment and deciding what furniture needed to be assembled first (my desk, apparently.) I know they happened because I have the evidence that they did. It is the only reason I am able to fill in some of the blanks from when my mind went absent.

Looking back to that part of the week, thinking about it, writing about it, even now it evokes an urge to keep moving.

I'm not a psych major. I barely feel like an English major at this point, when my words feel as disjointed as my mind. I imagine it has something to do with an intrinsic desire to outrun my past.

I woke up on Monday feeling fine and had returned from coffee feeling broken without fully grasping why. Memories were catching up to me in my periphery and there was this compulsion to keep pressing forward at all costs so they couldn't drag me backward.

The denial was still strong.

Who was Tanya to me, really?

Somewhere in the haze of frantically trying to assemble my perfect life with the perfect boyfriend who didn't know I was broken, I decided she was no one.

We'd only ever had one class together, back in high school. We'd only spoken a few times. She wasn't an old friend. I'd barely call her an acquaintance. I was desperate to believe the woman she'd become meant nothing to me.

Yet I saw her bruises in the shadows as I worked. I was driven half to madness by the memory of the gold that encompassed her ring finger. I saw the color of her eyes in the water as I tried to splash the fever from my face.

Those are the things, all the things, I have left from Monday afternoon. I remember bits and pieces of remembering her.

The last vivid recollection I have of the day was the phone call.

I'm a text person. Maybe it's my generation. Maybe it's my love of the written word. But I never call. I almost didn't recognize the sound my phone made for a ring. It was hideous. It may have snapped me out my haze, but I wanted more than anything for it to stop, and so I quickly went to hunt down the device.

My intention was to decline. To put it on silent. To shut off the phone so it couldn't make that sound anymore. That plan changed when I saw who was calling.

It was Eric.

He had never called me before, and I remember thinking it was an emergency. Suddenly my thoughts were clear as I answered, my mind going into crisis mode immediately. "Hello?"

"Hey, Mal." His voice was bright, cheerful. There was no emergency. I sighed in relief, and did not fully understand the sinking of my heart. He sounded as happy and as natural as if we spoke this way every day of our relationship.

"Why are you calling?" I asked.

We texted. We *always* texted. Hell—everyone did. To be talking to him over the phone was more annoying than I cared to admit.

"I just wanted to see how you were doing." There was a pause. "How are you doing?"

"Fine." I lied.

I didn't feel fine. My mouth was dry, and tasted of bile. My body felt weak and sweaty and it was all I could do to keep the phone lifted to my ear.

"Did I catch you in the middle of something?"

"I was just putting together my new desk."

"Should I leave you to it?"

"Yeah, probably."

I didn't like the way I sounded, or how I was talking to him. We didn't fight often, and this was approaching as cold as we'd ever spoken to one another. I didn't want to push him away. I wanted the opposite. I wanted him to be there with me, before I had to go through something terrible alone. In lack of that, I guess I just didn't want him to see how badly I needed him.

"Okay," he said. It hurt a little how he didn't sound hurt by my uncharacteristic rudeness. "Mal?"

"What?"

"You sure you're okay?"

It was an opportunity to make nice, and I forced myself to take it, despite the irrational annoyance that overtook me.

At first, I didn't know how.

The fear came bubbling up so strongly as I thought about explaining, that I was afraid I'd cry. That was another thing I didn't do: cry. Not in front of him, not ever in my adult life. What would he think if I did? How would I ever explain? Suddenly the space between us didn't feel like space anymore, it felt like a void. An abyss. It was something to drown in.

"Mal?"

I realized time had passed. Significant time apparently, where I had not answered.

I had to say something, for I was afraid I truly would sob if I had to endure another moment of the silence. "I'm just not feeling too well."

It was the wrong thing to say. I don't get sick often, and I didn't know how to accurately explain what was happening, or make it seem like nothing.

"What's wrong?"

I felt guilty when I heard the concern in his voice. It felt unearned. "Nothing serious. Just...a little queasy, is all."

"Have you eaten?"

"I had breakfast."

"It's almost eight out there, isn't it?" He sounded alarmed.

I was alarmed too. He was right. I had no idea where the time had gone. It didn't feel like I'd gotten enough accomplished for it to be so late.

"I must have lost track of time," I said numbly. An understatement.

"Between the move and setting up the new place, you're probably just pushing yourself too hard."

"You're probably right."

I wanted to kiss him. Once again, I wished he was there beside me so that I could. He had provided a rational explanation to my illness I could latch onto, if only for the time being.

I felt I could slip back into denial for a respite.

"I feel awful I'm not there. I wish it was next month."

"So do I."

"Soon. Very soon. So don't try to do everything without me, okay? Only the essentials. I'll help you get everything set up when I get out there."

"Okay."

"Go get some food, okay?"

"Okay."

"And promise me you won't push yourself too hard?"

"I promise."

For as much comfort as the impromptu call had given me, I felt desperate for it to come to an end. The false hope of his explanation had given me enough reprieve to actually feel my exhaustion.

"I love you, get some rest."

"I love you," I repeated numbly. His words crashed around me, hitting in a way they never had before.

I didn't eat anything when the call ended. The mere thought of food had my stomach all in knots.

Though I had never broken a promise to Eric before, I did push myself just a little harder. I forced my body, tired and sweaty though it was, to look for the cheap bed frame. When the thought of that became too tiresome, I settled for dragging the mattress into the bedroom and letting it fall onto the floor with a dull thud.

I briefly tried to find our sheets, before that too became too much of a chore. I settled for a few towels tossed on top of the mattress in a makeshift nest, which I was eager to curl up in.

Sleep found me easier than I had feared, though I was none too grateful for the gifts it brought.

Nightmare

HIM.

Me.

Teeth. His.

Breathing.

His. Mine.

None.

A smile.

His.

Tuesday (Before Dawn)

I WOKE UP IN a cold sweat, facing the wrong way. I don't know how else to describe it, besides to say I felt backward. Nothing about my surroundings made the slightest amount of sense.

I looked around for Lizzie.

Not only did I not find her, but there were no sheets. There was no handmade quilt from her grandmother pressing down on me, keeping me warm and compressed and calm.

And why did I expect there would be?

My eyes took their sweet time adjusting to the darkness, but when they did I could see my apartment. It was where I was supposed to live with Eric, but he wasn't there yet. I'd just had a nightmare.

It was one I'd had once before, back in college. The fear and confusion must have sent me back there, to my time with a different partner.

I don't remember my other encounter with the dream being so vivid—hadn't woken up where I could smell his breath or feel the bruise forming where his teeth had sunk into my arm. I had just woken up in her bed, sweating, confused, and breathing heavily enough to wake her.

Lizzie had brought me water and rubbed my back as she had eased me back to bed under the covers. I hadn't thought about her, or especially that night, for years. Then, last Tuesday morning she wasn't there to bring me water or ask if I had a history of night terrors, or rub my back sweetly until I was lulled to sleep once more. And I missed her. I had never thought about how good she was to me until she was gone—and even then, not for a long time after.

To tell you the sad truth of it, I couldn't remember why she left me at the time.

I had a feeling, as I curled up in my bed alone, that it had something to do with that nightmare. How I had acted after.

I had felt so uncomfortable in the last couple weeks of our relationship. I didn't want to be around someone who knew the truth about me, that I was vulnerable. That I was human. Even though I can't remember who said what, or when the last time we spoke was, I know without a doubt *I* was the one to chase *her* away.

Eventually we had a conversation that would be our last, and I would never see her warm smile, or her pink hair, or the vibrant quilt ever again.

I should apologize to Lizzie too, but that's another matter entirely.

What you need to know now is that on Tuesday morning, while the sun was coming up, I was tangled up in a nest of towels on my mattress, which I hadn't even gotten on top of the box spring.

It was as lonely as I'd been in a long time. Eric felt very far away.

I told myself that I missed him, and that I'd feel better if he were lying next to me. Honestly, though, I was glad he wasn't. If he had to comfort me back to sleep from a waking nightmare, he would be just another person out there in the world who knew I was weak. I didn't want to lose him like I had lost the others, proving a point to myself that I was strong.

I tried to think of something that wasn't the embrace of a man or woman that could lull me back to sleep. I didn't want to risk that dream again, but neither was I ready to be up. There was something eerie about an empty place in the dark of morning, when the pale light is just considering making its first appearance.

I reached for my phone, thinking maybe I could find a podcast to listen to while my heart stilled.

It only added more panic to the equation when I saw there were three missed calls, and three messages.

I was frantically reaching to listen to them, worried that it was Eric again, that he had been in an accident. When I saw it was from a Leyton area code, my finger froze.

Everyone I wanted to hear from in this town was in my phone. The missed calls and the messages alike were all part of the nightmare I was sinking into. Keeping that in mind, I deleted them all before I could think better of it, and was all too happy to put down the device.

Uneasily I closed my eyes and tried to picture orange slice quilts, only to be met with the mental image of a golden ring.

I tried to picture the next scene, by which I mean the first scene, in my book. This was often the technique I used to lull myself to my happy place, where I am a writer at my desk, and my only concern in the world is how the words fit together on the page.

It almost worked. It would have surely worked, were it not for the sound.

Footsteps.

They started in the hall and I could hear the weight shifting across my floorboards, drawing ever closer to the open door of this unfamiliar bedroom. I heard the soft squeak of a shoe just outside the doorframe, just outside my field of vision.

There was no getting back to sleep after that.

I sat there for a long time, holding my breath, waiting for another sound. After a while I even hoped for it to come closer, just so that I could prove I wasn't losing my mind.

All my patience was met with nothing but the faltering light of dawn, which illuminated the deep purple bruise forming on my forearm.

Tuesday (Continued)

I WAS EXHAUSTED. I had already been up for longer than I'd been asleep by the time I had the coffee pot set up—and still no grounds. Not to mention that what little slumber I'd gotten had been far from restful.

But I was productive all the same.

Between the bruise on my arm and the suspicion that someone—something—had been in my apartment, I was desperate for anything else to occupy my mind for a while.

Morning two of my perfect, year-long writer's retreat and the routine I had planned for myself was already put out to pasture. In fact, I could think of nothing I wanted to do less that morning than sit around with my thoughts. I sure as hell wasn't about to go back to that coffee shop.

So I spent the morning consciously doing the work that my body had started the day before without me. I made the apartment more livable. With a 90s alternative playlist blaring from my phone, I set up the few appliances we had brought and dug through boxes for a fresh T-shirt and clean underwear. I relished my short shower before making a trip to the corner store.

They didn't have a wide selection, but I found coffee grounds, filters, a box of cereal, and some basic sandwich supplies that I thought would be more than enough to tide me over while I figured some stuff out. On impulse, I also picked up a twelve back of ginger ale to keep around in case my stomach wanted to start acting up as it had the day before.

I bought it, but my plan was to continue the trend of feeling better.

That spirit was easier to maintain than the forced optimism of the day before. The bar for myself had been significantly lowered. In that respect, I was pleased just to get the bed set up properly and to call in for help setting up my internet. It was blissfully normal to be occupied.

Even the bad news of the day seemed like a relief for its potential to distract. It arrived in the form of an unexpected, one word text from CeCe.

One word.

Busted.

Tuesday (Evening)

I APPRECIATED THE HELL out of CeCe for giving me a head's up.

Two unexpected phone calls in two consecutive days (not counting the three I had promptly deleted in a panic) would have been too much for my anxiety riddled brain to handle, distraction or no.

With a warning in advance, however, I had about twenty minutes to mentally prepare myself for the incoming call from my mother.

I can't say it went well.

"When were you planning on telling me you were back in town?"

"When do I get to meet this boyfriend? The wedding?"

"Did you really think you could just traipse back home and I wouldn't notice?"

"Thank heavens CeCe told me, or I might have found out on Facebook. Facebook, for Christ's sake, Mallory."

"I pay for your damned phone bill, the least you could do is use it to tell me what state you're in."

"Dinner, tomorrow at 7:30."

These were just the highlights from about thirty minutes of incessant lecture. All in all, it could have gone a lot worse.

The first thing to understand about my mother is that it can always go worse, and more often than not, it does. When she's really angry, that's when she expects answers, and nothing I say will ever be to her satisfaction.

This performative anger is another beast entirely. Believe it or not, it requires less energy on the part of the disappointment to just sit on one end of the phone and acknowledge, every so often, that while the questions are all rhetorical, I'm still there. I'm still listening. In a weird way, the phone call was at least enough to assure me that one thing in Leyton had not changed.

Plus, this time around, I had to admit she had some valid points.

My mother can—and has—gone off about nearly everything. She was upset about my major, she was upset about the college I chose, the fact I didn't ask her for help with the application, how I wore my hair, what my dreams were. She was such a bright and sunny person to everyone else around her, it often feels like all that's left for me is her disapproval.

This time, I deserved the lecture. And her disappointment.

In my defense, such as it is, I had meant to tell her I'd be moving back. The week leading up to the move I had spent so much time figuring out how to approach the subject that I had run out of time to actually do it. The plan after that had been to show up at the house, make the move out to be a last-minute affair, and give her a bottle of wine so she could see an effort had been made. I figured there would be less drama if I were the one to make the first move. I'd meant to do it Monday, but then *Monday* had happened.

Despite the failure on my end, and generally being a bad daughter, this ordeal was one of the highlights of my week.

In the twenty minutes between when CeCe had texted me and when Mom had called, I had been so stressed about the impending rebuke that I hadn't even thought of the other strangeness going on in my life. In the thirty minutes of lecture, I hadn't thought about it much either. Though I knew a dinner at my mother's house the following day would be filled with admonishments from her, the thought of having plans outside the apartment where I would not be able to run into anyone unexpected didn't sound so bad. Thinking about it during the ten minutes where I made and ate my sandwich rounded out the time to a full hour of the day where I didn't think about Tanya once.

How quickly these little relative troubles are put into perspective when we fear something dark may be afoot.

Yes, Tuesday was, relatively speaking, a good day.

I was feeling so elated, in fact, that once I'd gotten off the phone and eaten, I sat my tablet on my new desk and I began to work on my first chapter.

Are you familiar with the "planner vs pantser" idea, my dear hypothetical reader?

It describes two different types of writers. The ones who outline and plan their drafts, in contrast the ones who just fly in by the seat of their pants. Most writers identify quite strongly with one of these methods over the other.

I spent much of my college career learning to be better at planning so I could meet the deadlines set before me.

There are things that are easier with an outline, for sure.

Academically speaking, when you're writing arguments and trying to make certain citation quotas, planning thoroughly can shave hours off the process. Even in short fiction writing (and again, especially with deadlines) something as simple as a list of bullet points can stop a blank page from staring back at you. It can get the creative juices flowing while also providing structure.

That's what I don't like about it—the structure.

I like a chance to see where my characters take me, what they would do organically had I not already decided how much time is allotted for them to get from point A to point B. Where do they *want* to go? How would they react if I had no agenda? I think that's where most of my realism comes from—from those early drafts where I try to imagine people interacting as honestly as I can.

But there is a price to pay for this.

More editing. More rewrites. More pieces of scrap paper with technical questions and things to look up later. There are notes to myself to make sure that the timelines add up by the time it has all been condensed and cleaned and changed.

Of course, that isn't an issue when you're writing nonfiction. There are no fictional timetables to refer to, no technical questions, you just have to tell it like it happened. Sometimes that's harder. Often, it makes less sense.

I feel myself now, getting lost in these memories. It's hard, sitting down to tell it all at once. To stay focused.

For a normal project, sometimes you would have to go back and change all the extra thoughts so that it's tidy and consistent, and paced better than you were able to wing on the spot.

In life, we don't always get to go back.

I should get some sleep. It's light out now, I've typed through the night, and I'm rambling.

I'll finish this section, and then I'll go to bed, beside my ghost for one more night. Tomorrow I'll finish. Tomorrow will be another chance to sleep alone. For now, I just want to finish this chapter.

What I was trying to say, before I got lost, before I started rambling about writing techniques, is that it was nice to play pretend. My imaginary playground was back, and it was full of friends, and I enjoyed getting lost in a stream of consciousness for a little while.

Tuesday morning I felt like my imagination was running a bit too wild. I liked the feeling of letting it roam constructively for a while, even if the draft was messy and terrible.

It was paced poorly. I ranted some. The characters repeated themselves with unnecessary dialogue. I told more than I showed. I didn't describe the setting as vividly as I meant to.

I remember being self-conscious about the style, as well.

A lot of writing quirks can be forgiven if the author knows how to write in a style that's appropriate for the story they want to tell. I want my book to fall in the realm of magical realism. The pains of modern society meet the wonder of the unexplained. That wasn't how it read, yet, but I fancied myself that there were seeds of such a story, waiting to be cultivated.

My favorite author is actually Jane Austen. When it comes to plot I look to the more modern, Hoffman, Atwood, the occasional Gaiman. But there are few things quite so beautiful as the way Austen could string her sentences together. It may well have been a sign of her era, but I believe her eloquence remains, to this day, unmatched.

It's a style of prose I have often tried to emulate in my work.

When I'm writing naturally, though, sharing my thoughts as they really are, in my own style, it's not half so lovely, is it?

My sentences get short. Or too long, sometimes, rambling and raving with no natural conclusion in sight. Improper. I see things in such terrible fragments.

This is an ugly little story I'm telling you, I suppose. It's been an ugly little week.

I think I have a rough night ahead of me.

I will depart now, for whatever sleep I can manage to get before this deed is done. But in the interest of keeping my word, and laying it all out, ugly thoughts and all, I have one more quick confession before I go.

I often think, despite my best wishes, that mine is a voice better suited to horror.

Intermission

Books don't normally have intermissions, do they? Then again, this isn't really a book, I suppose.

This is just a *thing* I need to write, so my ghost may take her leave of me.

I'm feeling better today. I caught up on some much needed sleep. I stood in the boiling water of a shower until the last traces of blood were gone. I ate. I ate a lot.

Doing all those things before I wrote goes against the shiny routine I had set for myself, and yet my resolve is stronger than ever.

I need to get back to this.

My name is Mallory Brennan.

It is so late into Sunday that the calendar on my phone, wherever it is, will soon read "Mon".

I have a little post-it note on my desk with bullet points of what the next fourteen chapters will contain.

I'm determined to finish this, and I did a little outline to save time.

While mulling over all the people I have wronged in my life, I decided to spare a thought to anyone who stumbles across this.

I have no choice but to continue. You, on the other hand, hypothetical reader, may turn back. This will be your last warning to do so.

My next break in the story is the epilogue. But don't worry. You'll be mentioned there whether you see it or not.

This next chapter is a nightmare.

Nightmare

HIM.

Me.

Teeth scrape against my skin and then clamp down.

His teeth are *in* me.

My breathing gets involuntarily heavy.

His heart races.

As does mine.

He waits for my reaction, so I give him none.

A smile.

His.

Wednesday (Morning)

It had not been done so easily, going to sleep, knowing the nightmares may come back, but I had felt so good the evening of, and I had been so very tired.

I was sweating into proper sheets that morning, and I knew better than to look for Lizzie.

I had remembered why we had broken up—what had started it, at least. Many such memories were coming back to me, though I would sooner have left them in the past.

Lizzie was the first girl I had dated in college. That made her special. With all two of the girls I'd dated in high school, it felt almost *performative*. It wasn't that I didn't like them, or want them, it was that I wanted to show off how much I was fine. I wasn't trying to build anything. What was there to build when all I wanted was away?

With Lizzie, it was different. I liked being with her all the time, and not just because she was pretty. She was smart, and charming and knew completely who she was. She was my fresh start in a new place and quickly she became a little piece of my identity as a new person, away from my decaying hometown.

I'm sure everyone feels this way about their first healthy relationship, but being with her made me believe we would last forever. I wasn't in love with her, exactly, but I was in love with the way I felt *around* her. At least that's how it was at first.

It was an offhand comment she made. She was smiling when she told me. "Aw! Some rando on Facebook is getting married."

It would have been harmless if I hadn't glanced over. If I hadn't seen his face on her phone.

Married.

"How do you know him?"

"I don't really. He's in some sort of game group with my cousin's ex." She did a double take when she saw my expression. "How do *you* know him?"

I forced a smile that looked more natural than it felt. I was in better practice then. "From high school."

"From Ohio?"

It was weird she didn't know that. Then again, maybe it wasn't. I hadn't exactly been forthcoming about details from my past. Things were sliding out from underneath me, and I did my best to make a joke about it. "You didn't think I was a local, did you?"

"Do you know the bride, too?" Time slowed. I couldn't play cool and beg her not to tell me who it was. I couldn't do both at the same time. I was so in the habit of being fine that I chose wrong, and I let her ask the next, inevitable part of the question where she would tell me the name of the woman I had condemned with my secrets. "Tanya Grace?"

There it was.

"I think I may have had a class with her, once."

It was German. We were the only two sophomores taking it, with a handful of seniors, over the more popular French and Spanish courses. I remembered it vividly. I remembered *her* vividly.

As I said, she resonated.

She was charming, and self-assured, and effortlessly talented in everything she did. She fit in naturally wherever she was, and her ambitions, whatever they might have been, were entirely her own. She shared little of herself, but there was always so much emotion behind such expressive eyes.

We spoke a few times, mostly in awkward conversations that lacked our mother tongue. Mostly using our German pseudonyms, which we had taken for the class.

"Ich bin Tammen. Du bist?"

"Hallo Tammen. Ich bin Marlena."

Even now, I can see her perfectly—and not just the ghost atop my dresser, smiling at this admission. I can also see the teenage Tanya, conjugating her verbs. I can almost make out the faded song lyrics on her red sneakers.

That was how I lost Lizzie.

I played it cool for the rest of the conversation, and I left, and I had a hard day practicing the art of being fine. I slept with her one more time, and I woke up in a cold sweat, and even though she was good to me, she'd seen the terrible secret I was hiding.

I wasn't fine.

I was vulnerable.

I was human.

After that, it felt as though I had to compensate, so I played even cooler. So cool in fact, that we lost all contact. I didn't let myself think too hard about that loss. She was beginning to see through me. I would have lost her in the end anyway.

That's what I tell myself, at least.

That's what makes it bearable. Last Wednesday, I realized there was more in my life that needed to be bearable, if I was to continue going.

When I was younger I was worried sick that my silence would cost someone more than what I had ever lost. The guilt used to keep me up, until I learned to live with it. When I found out who had paid the price, I learned to live with *that* too.

Until last Monday when we had crossed paths.

My first day back to town, and I came face to face with the embodiment of my deepest regret.

Maybe there is no such thing as coincidence.

It is harder than you can imagine, in this big wide world, to cut someone out of your life or to end up away from where you started. When I moved out West I didn't think I'd fall for someone who would get a paid internship in the middle of nowhere, where I had grown up. I didn't think my first girlfriend would be cousins with someone who dated someone who played Xbox games with the man who had nearly destroyed me. I never thought that man would get married, or that I'd ever hear about it if he did. What were the chances that his wife was working at the closest coffee shop to my new place, right when I happened to arrive?

None of it seems random to me anymore, but that wasn't what I was telling myself earlier in the week. Wednesday morning, I was ready to be done with all the strangeness, and put the whole ordeal to bed however I could.

I was just about to get up for the day when I heard the weight shifting on the floor again. This time my bedroom door was closed, and I could see the shadows of someone pacing just outside.

In the movies, they go to investigate these impossible specters. I went to take a shower. I was more than prepared to go face Tanya, but I was not inviting any more scary shit into my life. Not willingly. Not Wednesday.

It worked.

As it always does, denial worked for a brief time.

My refusal to investigate the shadow, or listen to the mysterious phone messages before deleting them, or talk about the strange sounds, it was all turning out just fine.

By the time I was showered and dressed, I was pleased to see there was nothing under my bedroom door. It left me free and clear to do what I thought would work. It left me a window to try and do the right thing.

I headed straight for The Northern Grind.

It was every bit as crowded, noisy, and obnoxious as I'd given it credit for on the first visit. This was clearly not an opinion shared by the man behind the counter who seemed enraptured by the music. I had to raise my voice just to place my order, which didn't mesh with the friendly demeanor I was aiming to impersonate.

"One cup of the house blend, please. Black."

He rang me up, though he seemed more interested in the drums of the track that was playing than delivering me my beverage. I wanted nothing more than to leave him to it, but I was not to be deterred.

"Hey, by the way, do you happen to know a woman working here? Tanya?"

He stopped moving his head to the music and met my eyes warily.

I kept going. "Blonde? Blue eyes? A little taller than me?"

Wariness turned to outright suspicion along his face. "You know her?"

"I'm an old friend from high school. I heard she works here?"

"She did."

"Did?"

He shrugged. "She never showed up for her shift yesterday. Didn't call in or anything. The manager is pretty pissed."

I remembered, unfortunately, the sound of my floorboards creaking on Tuesday morning. This time I envisioned red canvas shoes creeping closer.

I couldn't allow myself to believe that's truly where she had been. It wasn't possible. It didn't make any sense.

I scribbled down my number on one of the stiff napkins and handed it to the barista. I am not in the habit of distributing my phone number so carelessly, but I was approaching the state of desperate rationalization that overrode my caution. This was what *had* to be done. More than anything I needed to see Tanya, in the flesh, with my own two eyes.

Then we could talk. When I saw her, it could end.

"If she comes in, would you tell her to call me?"

"And what did you say your name was?"

"Mal. Mallory Brennan. She'll know me."

Of that much, I was certain. I still believed there was something to be done for her—that I would do whatever it took.

Even I was surprised at the lengths I would truly go to.

Wednesday (Dinner)

I FELT JITTERY ON the drive.

The several cups of caffeine coursing through my veins may well have been an appropriate place to lay some of that blame. I preferred to think of it as my body rejecting the very idea of visiting my mother.

Not to mention, I had other valid reasons to be on edge.

I kept trying to tell myself to forget it. It was irrational to think that Tanya not being at work had anything to do with me. I didn't know her anymore, if you could ever say I really *knew* her in the first place. She'd been living a life all these years, like me, and there could be a million other things going on. A million reasons why she was suddenly gone.

But it wasn't working.

I could feel it in my bones—something bad had happened. She was haunting me. Even driving, I could hear the creaking footsteps that had echoed in my apartment. I knew they were made by the red Converse shoes of my ghost.

No matter what I did to try and keep my focus on the road, on the dinner, my mind kept painting the picture of what had happened. I became increasingly certain there had been a murder. He had killed her, because of me, and now I was being haunted.

"No," I whispered to myself. "She's alive. Just two days ago, I *saw* her."

I could not shake the feeling that I had been the last innocent person to see her alive, and I was starting to not feel so innocent. It was actually a relief to find myself on the porch of the old house, despite the bittersweet nature of the memories that awaited.

I didn't know whether or not to knock. The bones of the house were still the same, still the shape of the house I had grown up in. It would have been my right to enter, but that felt like a long time ago. I had changed so much, as had every external feature of the home. I'd become a stranger.

It was no longer the soft cream I had known, but a bright yellow with alternating shades of red and orange in the trim, and pink curtains. The whole place looked like a pack of Starbursts. The old wooden swing had been replaced with modern, abstract metal furniture, all of which was swarming with cats.

I rang the doorbell and was met with nothing. I knocked.

"Hello?" I called.

The only response I got was the derisive meows from the silver tabbies weaving between my legs.

I checked my watch which told me I was right on time—save for the few minutes I had spent staring at the house and waiting for a response. Finally, I just tried the door. It was unlocked, and I was escorted in by several of the felines as I made my way through to the kitchen, where my mother was waiting to toss them little scraps of meat.

"Why were you out there winding them up?" She snapped at me.

That was more or less the welcome I should have expected.

"I wasn't winding them up, I was calling for you. No one answered the door."

"You could have come right in. You know I never lock up."

Never mind the fact I did not feel welcomed to do so. "You really ought to. This isn't a good neighborhood."

I didn't mention that with the garish paint job, the neighbors may well feel she was flaunting some kind of imagined wealth—if they weren't too busy thinking of her as the crazy cat lady.

"It's a fine neighborhood. Go set the table."

It occurred to me as I followed her instructions, that perhaps not all of the wealth *was* imagined. The plates were kept in the same place, but they were nicer than the ones I remember eating from when I lived there. They all matched, for one thing, and seemed to be made of a very nice ceramic.

The wine glasses were nice too. The silverware had been replaced. The home was still erratic, and cluttered, but her attention seemed to be on finer things. As far as I knew, she was still working for less than minimum wage at the women's shelter, which meant CeCe's practice must have finally taken off. I held onto that hope like a life raft, knowing that mother would want to brag and I could take the attention off myself.

"Where's Cecelia?" I asked.

Mom brought in a big pan filled with spinach ravioli that I *hoped* was vegan. I knew better than to ask.

"She got held up at work, so she'll be late."

That didn't come as welcome news.

I poured the wine while Mom dished out the pasta and salad, and the store-bought bread she always took the time to heat up in the oven. It wasn't a bad meal, but I drank deeply before trying my first bite.

I was not well, and was in no mood for the onslaught of conversation with my mother without CeCe running interference.

To my surprise, she didn't comment on my drinking. Or my hair, which she liked for me to wear longer than I do. She didn't say much of anything at first, just took a big drink from her glass.

The taste of the bread made me nostalgic. It made me miss when Dad was at these dinners. That was a topic I knew was off limits, and I was the first to break the silence, if only to stop thinking about it. "The food's great."

"I didn't know what to make, or what you're eating these days. You look thin. Are you settling in okay?"

I was surprised by her concern, not yet realizing it for the trap it was. I should have known better.

"Yeah, I'm settling in just fine."

"You could have told me, you know."

"I was actually wondering how you found out."

It wasn't what I had meant to say, or how I'd meant for it to sound. The question had been nagging at me on some back-burner of my brain, and I had blurted it out in a way that had come across as accusatory. CeCe hadn't mentioned *how* I had been busted though, and I was curious.

From my mother's expression, I could tell exactly how my inquiry into the matter had landed. There were Oscar winners incapable of my mother's performance. She looked as if I had shot her with my statement—this woman who had never called to check on me a single time while I had been away.

"Is it so dreadful here that you must actively ignore me, Mallory?" she whined. "It's bad enough you forgot to tell me you were coming home, but to conspire against me knowing..." she trailed off as she shook her head in silent disapproval.

Already, I wanted to scream at her to just stop being so dramatic. To stop being so hypocritical. I was able to catch myself. "I was just *curious*. I was planning to surprise the two of you once I had settled in, I was wondering what ruined that."

I could tell from the look on her face that she didn't believe me, but that she had no intention of calling me out on the little half-truth. What she wanted—what she had always wanted more than an actual relationship between us—was a good story about our interactions. A tall tale about a ruined surprise might be even more satisfactory than if I had remembered to tell her. After a moment considering this, she calmed down enough to answer my question. "Gabriel just happened to mention it."

The name made my blood run cold.

I didn't know which of the terrible things was worst.

Hearing his name, on its own, was enough to make me feel as though I'd been run through with an icicle. The casual manner in which she said it was just as bad. There was also the implication that they had stayed in touch. It all made me sick.

Literally.

I barely made it through the back door in time to vomit over the side of the deck. I felt like I'd had too much to drink, more than the one deep swallow of wine that had come up with my bread. My vision was blurry. My head spun. It took several, foul-tasting breaths before I could feel the rest of my body.

I didn't know that he could have such a strong effect on me, still. I hated that just hearing his name could do that.

It felt so surreal, once I had collected myself, to go back in and seat myself at the table across from my mother's appraising look. "You aren't pregnant, are you?"

"God, Mom, no."

"Are you sure? Sometimes you don't know straight away."

"I'm not."

"Do you use protection?"

"Mom! Stop. I'm not pregnant. It's just a migraine."

She got up and brought me a tall glass of water, with two translucent blue gel pills. I took them without further information.

"I get those, sometimes." Her tone was low, almost concerned.

"Worse than before?"

She sighed, and took more of her wine. "Not as often. But they're just as bad."

"Have you been to the doctor?"

She gave me another withering gaze. "You sound just like your father. And CeCe. You know how I feel about doctors."

"You should take care of yourself."

"You're one to talk, Mallory."

I wanted to point out that my symptoms had only just started—and I didn't even have a doctor lined up in Ohio yet. What good would it have done, though? I knew there were more important, albeit more painful things to discuss. Despite my upset stomach, I washed the water and the pills down with more wine in preparation.

"You said Gabriel talked to you?"

I was surprised at how steady my voice sounded, even as the rest of me was spinning out of control.

"Yes, he did. I see him around sometimes. He said you ran into his wife on Monday."

The well of my denial was beginning to dry up.

"How did she look? His wife, I mean."

"You're the one who saw her, Mallory. Not me."

"You mean... She wasn't with him when he bumped into you?"

I shouldn't have been as surprised as I felt—especially since I didn't believe it was a coincidence he was running into my mother on a semi-regular basis.

"No. Why do you ask?"

"She just... She looked thin when I saw her...and she..."

She's haunting me? For a weird, drastic moment, I almost confided this to my mother. It wasn't because I trusted her, or even thought that she would care. She was just the only person I knew who believed in anything spiritual or ghostly.

"She what, Mallory?"

Mother looked so annoyed and impatient with me, that I came to my senses quickly about wanting to tell her.

"She rushed out pretty quickly, was all."

"I don't blame her."

I panicked then. I wondered what he'd told her in the years I'd been gone, if she knew why we broke up, or some twisted version of it. She seemed to believe I had something to feel guilty for, to scare away Tanya. "Why do you say that?"

"Well, you know."

"Tell me."

"You're probably the only person who could steal her husband away from her." It was all I could do not to retch again, but my mother didn't stop. "I've never seen a boy so much in love."

I don't know how I kept the bile down. I taste it again, typing those words. "Eric loves me."

I don't know if I was saying that for her benefit, or for mine.

"I never said he didn't. But Gabriel..."

"I've gotta go, Mom." I was up, with my purse in hand so quickly that I didn't hear all of her protestations. I knew if I didn't go immediately I'd end up puking again, right there on the table.

I passed CeCe on my way out.

"Hey, Mal. Wh—"

"Sorry, CeCe," I moved past her as quickly as I could. "I'm running really late. We'll talk later."

"Talk later then."

No doubt she thought I'd gotten into another fight with my mother. I didn't care in that moment. All I could think about was getting home and getting into bed.

I so desperately needed the rest.

Wednesday (Continued)

BUT REST WOULD NOT find me.

It wouldn't come after I had sweated my way through another scalding hot shower, or when I curled up in my bed. I just couldn't stop thinking about her, or the timeline.

I see her.

She's bruised.

She runs from me.

She tells her husband.

She goes missing.

He tells my mom.

It all seemed to point to what I already knew to be the truth—Tanya Grace was *haunting* me.

The only thing I couldn't prove was that she had gone missing. Or worse. One missed day of work didn't mean much. I didn't *know* she was dead. I thought if I could prove it, or better yet *disprove* it, I could get the whole thing out of my mind and get some sleep.

I cracked open one of my ginger ales and opened Facebook. It was the only place I could think of that I might know where to find her online. Unfortunately, it didn't take long to discover that her account was private.

I beat myself up for a while, wondering if I should send an invite so I could check. Even if I did, she'd probably reject it. Then she'd have proof I was looking her up.

It would be a step backward, no matter how I looked at it.

A nasty thought hit me.

She was friends with him.

I knew his password.

I couldn't confirm it was the same, not unless I tried, but I knew he was a man set in his ways. He was still meeting my mother, after all. He was obviously still thinking about me.

It would be easy enough to try the login, just to see.

The thought was awfully tempting. It wouldn't take much to convince myself she was still alive. A status update. A photo. A comment. Hell, even a *like* would prove that I was overreacting. Then I could stop scaring myself and go to bed. I *needed* to get to bed.

I made it as far as logging out of my own account and typing in his email before I thought better of it.

What I was doing was creepy. Wrong. Invasive.

It would also be akin to an invitation. It felt like it would be opening a door to him to let him further back into my life.

I imagined him getting the email notification saying someone had signed into his account from a new device. I could see him sitting there, at his computer, smiling, knowing that I was back in Leyton and he was back under my skin already.

I decided I would not be giving him the satisfaction.

So I closed my tablet and resigned myself to a restless night wondering about Tanya, half-expecting to hear her footsteps.

I would have taken that over the dream.

Wednesday (Night)

My dream that night was more vivid than I had ever dreamed, and far different than my recurring nightmare. It was less abstract.

I didn't wake up with bruises after, but I almost would have preferred that to the inescapable detail of what I was seeing.

It feels too personal to even talk about.

But I suppose this entire thing has been.

And with her eyes still upon me, I am afraid to leave anything out. They were prominent in my dream as well, only they were larger than life as they judged me.

It took longer than I would have liked to have control over myself, to be able to pull back. When I did, I could see it was not just her eyes that were larger than life, but her entire face. I'd been standing very, very close to a picture of her from the waist up. She was wearing a dress with an old-fashioned white lace collar. Her lips were upturned into a smile that didn't reach those cold, blue eyes. There was her iconic braid, swept up into a bun with the rest of her hair.

The photograph was cropped awkwardly so that it caught just the corner of a man's shoulder beside her.

A wedding photo, I realized, only that wasn't quite right. The way he'd been cropped out, the size of it, the texture of the paper, it felt all wrong.

I glanced around to the rest of the room, my stomach sinking as I put it all together. I saw the pews first, then the stained-glass windows, and finally the coffin.

I was at Tanya Grace's funeral.

I was almost angrier about the photo they had used than I was about her death. Dream logic is just like that sometimes. I should have been sad for her, or angry at the wrongful death, but I was so caught up on what picture they had used. She wasn't being mourned as a person, as Tanya, but forever remembered in that somber photo as his wife.

I hated it, but it was nothing compared to how I felt when I approached the casket and saw she was wearing that same, vintage lace garment to be buried in.

I could just make out the ring of purple bruises on her neck beneath the collar before the dream began to fade.

As reality swirled in, I was a flurry of emotions. I was furious, and sad, and certain that there would be no justice in the waking world. I did not think there would be a body, or a funeral, or any kind of closure where I might see her again.

But when I opened my eyes, she was sitting on the edge of my bed.

Thursday (Morning)

I SAID THAT I was not crazy this time last week. I don't believe I have lost touch with reality past the point of no return. I know all too well what I'm going through, what I've been experiencing.

If someone didn't believe me, or my story, however, and they wanted to pinpoint the exact moment in time that I started to crack, it would be at around 4:50 a.m., Thursday morning.

She has hardly left my side since she first appeared, and even I can't believe how *real* she seems to me sometimes. How real she seems right *now*.

At first, I didn't know what to think, what to make of her presence.

I'd just woken, so I knew she wasn't a dream. I've never been afflicted with hallucinations, so I ruled that out rather quickly (though it's a theory I've revisited often in the last couple days.) Her visage was so eerie that it was hard to mistake her as a flesh and blood person, even while I was looking at her head on.

Still, I had to try something.

"Tanya?"

She smiled at me. It wasn't a sinister smile, exactly, but it was *unsettling*.

I pulled the blankets closer around my body.

I wanted nothing more than to curl up under the covers until all the monsters went away, like when I was a child. I wanted to believe more than anything she was something I could just sleep into nonexistence.

Only I didn't believe I could.

"What are you doing here?" I asked.

But I *knew*.

She was there to haunt me, like any good ghost would. Pretending to ignore her was not likely to make her go away. I would need to do all the other ghostly things. Learn the truth about her death. See justice brought. Repent to God. Confess my sins.

Without even thinking about how to do any of that, I rolled out of bed and got dressed as quickly as I could.

Had I not already accepted that the Tanya in my room was a ghost, I would have caught on from the way she followed me. It wasn't that she did follow me, it was *how* she did it. She didn't appear as fluid that first day as she appears to me now that she is stronger.

She didn't move much, didn't stand or walk, or shift around behind me. She was just always there, lingering in my periphery as I set about the day.

Her smile had faded rather quickly to a look of cold, calculation that focused on me as I headed for my car, where she was also somehow in the passenger's seat.

It was too early, I reckoned, for the coffee shop to have opened, so I found myself taking the long way around. The route took me past our old school.

I slowed the car to a crawl as I took in the sight of the old building. It looked just as outdated as I remember, but more dilapidated. I parked, and without even meaning to, I wasted the better part of an hour just staring at it. The beacon of hope for the town's future, where I had taken all my AP classes, crumbling away into disrepair.

It wasn't that the view brought back memories. It didn't. What it brought was a deep longing for all that might have been, for the four happy years I might have spent there had everything not gotten so twisted.

I watched the sky lighten to a milky gray, only vaguely aware of my growing despondency. The sounds of traffic starting up from somewhere behind me was enough to finally jolt my attention away from the void opening up from within.

I wanted to cry.

To let it all out.

But I felt more self-conscious in the light of day, and with my ghost still beside me. Hollow, I started up the car and headed back to The Northern Grind.

I don't know what I was hoping to find there, if I'm being perfectly honest with you.

I knew it wasn't going to be Tanya.

Maybe I was hoping for the police, or her mother, or a friend. Someone—anyone—who could come in looking for her. I wanted there to be people searching who might have meant more to her than I did.

The most I got was a suspicious stare from the same hipster barista I had questioned about her the day before.

What was he thinking? I wondered. Did he believe she was missing too? That I had something to do with it? Would he have been so wrong?

He kept shooting glances over my way, and I wondered if he couldn't see the ghost seated across from me. Before I grew wild enough to ask, I was saved by the ringing of my phone.

I answered, eager to talk to Eric, only it wasn't him.

"Mallory, are you busy?"

"Mother?"

"Yes, Mallory. Are you busy?"

Even in my strained condition and under the most unusual circumstances, I paused to consider if it was a trap. It could be, but what else would I say? Admitting that I was waiting around to see if Tanya came into work would do little but prove Mr. Man Bun right in his belief I was stalking her. Making up an excuse might just be an invitation to let her pry into my medical well-being, and ask me about pregnancy again.

"Mallory?"

We had only been on the phone for a minute and already she had used the full name three times.

"No, Mom. I'm not busy."

"Great. I could use your help down at the shelter."

"The shelter?"

"Yes, Mallory. The shelter. You remember it, don't you?"

She sounded exasperated with my constant need for repetition, but I was surprised. Of course I remembered the shelter. That was where I had done my compulsory volunteer hours before graduation. In a way, I had worked there before my mother, and I almost told her so before I thought better of it.

"I remember it. What sort of help do you need?"

"I'll tell you when you get down here." She paused. "You're not sick, are you?"

"Sick?"

"You were throwing up last night. Are you sure it's not contagious? We don't need any of the women catching it."

Again, the urge to snark was strong. Last night she had been convinced I was pregnant, and now she thought I was contagious. I wanted to point out that even if that were the case, she'd be just as likely to pass it to the women as I was at this point.

Honestly, I just didn't have the energy. "Yeah. I'm on my way."

I glanced to the chair across from me, but Tanya was already waiting by the exit. With a sigh, knowing she would be accompanying me, I followed her out.

Thursday (Continued)

I WAS MORE SURPRISED by how late it was in the day than I was by the dead girl in my car. I'd gotten to the coffee shop early in the morning, and somehow I wasn't leaving until almost 3 p.m.

Maybe *that's* why I had been getting strange looks from the barista.

It was the second instance that day of me losing time by just spacing the fuck out. I wasn't sleeping well, or eating right. I wasn't even sure if I could keep food down.

I checked my reflection in the rear-view mirror once I arrived, only to see that I looked about as shitty as I felt. I don't keep makeup in my car or purse, so there was little that could be done about the bags under my eyes or my general pallor. I didn't have a brush either.

The best I could do was smooth down my hair before pulling it up into a ponytail that felt more painful than perky, then pop a piece of mint chewing gum into my mouth. All the while, Tanya smirked at my efforts.

I tried to ignore her and look like a normal person as I headed into the women's shelter to find my mother. It, unlike my childhood home, looked exactly as I remembered.

The lights did the interior no favors, but there were a few plants, big windows, and the walls were papered over in the colorful paintings from children who no doubt wanted to make the best of their circumstances. In a way, this felt more like a homecoming than anything else in Leyton.

I still didn't know what I was doing there exactly, but I was grateful to be in surroundings so familiar, presumably about to do good work. It had been awhile since I'd gotten the opportunity to do any volunteering, a practice I had kept from high school into college until finals had rolled around. Contributing to something bigger than myself was not only rewarding, but had proven time and time again to be the most effective way of running from my demons—or ghosts, as the case may be.

When I first arrived, I had hope that the trip may be as beneficial to me as it would be to the shelter, or my mother. It didn't take long for such an expectation to sour in my mother's hands.

The way she introduced me was worse than anything I could have possibly conjured up.

In the grand scheme of things, with all else that was going on, it does not seem so terribly significant. But on Thursday, even in the thick of my haunting, it was enough to cut me deeply.

The beaming smile. The cooing of her voice. The false pride. I would have been as charmed as her coworkers by our relationship, had I never seen us together either. If I didn't know how she acted toward me behind closed doors.

It was not that she was outwardly hostile, or cruel, but there was constant disapproval, a constant indifference that bordered on malice between us.

It seemed she was only capable of loving me in front of an audience.

"Have you met my daughter Mallory?"

"I'm just so proud of my daughter."

"She's just graduated from college, you know."

"It's so good to have her home again after so long."

Bullshit.

It was all I could do not to call her out on her bullshit in front of all the friends she insisted on parading me around in front of. And for what? Was she so desperate to look like a good mother? She must have been, for she spent more time showing me to her associates and making introductions for me than she had spent actually talking to me in *years*. I was beginning to think it was the entire reason she'd called me down there, before it became apparent she did actually need my help with something.

It was nothing too strenuous, thankfully. Someone had called out sick, and she just needed assistance with unloading the new shipment of supplies. It gave me something to do at least, to get my mind off my angers as she failed to bait me into several conversations. I'd have looked like (and would probably have felt like) a monster had I stormed off after agreeing to help, but staying was all I could manage. I found I wasn't in a mood to play along with her happy family charade. I saw no reason why I should put in the effort, not in front of everyone, and especially not once it was just the two of us alone in the alley.

She was not so oblivious as to miss my irritation, but neither was she mature enough to address the issue head on.

I held my bitter silence. I let her squirm. I did her work while she tossed out vain scraps of conversation my way, like I was another one of her strays—the only one she didn't care much for. I was on track to win our little war, until one of her offhand comments pierced right through me.

"I saw Gabriel again today."

My reaction to his name was not as violent as it had been the night before, but it was enough to make my blood run cold, and it as good as forced me to ask for elaboration.

It was the closest thing I'd gotten on a lead to Tanya all day, and all but confirmed my theory that he was running into my mother on purpose.

"Do you usually see him this often?"

She didn't even consider my question, she just answered with a practiced ease that I took note of. I wondered how much of this conversation she had already planned out in her head. A more cynical part of me wondered if this was not the true reason she had asked me along in the first place.

"Not usually so often. I think he's hoping to run into you."

"I don't want to run into him," I told her firmly.

"I think it's sweet he still thinks about you after all these years."

"He has a wife, Mother." *Had a wife,* I thought.

"Marriages aren't always happy, Mallory."

It was simply too much. It broke me.

Part of me was horrified that on a surface level, this comment was made to push me back into the waiting arms of my married, abusive, asshole of an ex. Part of me was furious to know that beneath it, there was a jab at my father, who had always been too good to her by half. My father, who was dead, and could not defend himself. My father, who never would have put me in a situation like this.

I didn't mean to tell her. Not then. Not ever. But her comment broke me, and I slipped.

"He wasn't good to me."

She chuckled, and I wanted to slap her. "That boy spoiled you. I never—"

"He wasn't good to me," I repeated, louder. "And I wish you wouldn't talk to him."

She stopped what she was doing to look at me, to *really* look at me. I kept moving boxes, hoping it would keep my hands from shaking.

"You never said anything," she said at long last.

"I broke up with him," I countered. "It should have been enough."

"I just thought..."

"You thought wrong."

I had started the conversation, but letting such a great weight off my chest was enough for that day. I didn't want to engage further.

"If you had told me, I wouldn't have..." she trailed off on her own that time, and I didn't interrupt her. The enormity of such words, in such a place as we were standing, must have hit her hard. I could have let her off the hook, changed the subject, but I didn't know what to say. For the first time in my life, my mother surprised me.

"I'm sorry."

I inhaled sharply. "It's not okay," I told her bluntly. "But thank you."

We were almost out of boxes by the time she spoke again. "Have you talked to someone about this?"

Emboldened by the shift in sincerity between us, I spoke with more candor than I had known I could muster. "I'm dealing with it as best I can. That's all you need to know."

She nodded, and I saw a rare chance to push further.

"If you want to help me, if you want to make this right, you can start by promising me that you won't talk about this. Not to anyone."

I could all too clearly picture her at home, sobbing into CeCe's arms about how she didn't know, all the while being comforted over a tragedy *I* still had to bear the weight of.

She started to object. "Mallory, I—"

"It's my story, and I don't want it shared."

That part rang as hollow for me then as it does now. But it worked. For once, miraculously, she backed down. "I understand."

"Promise me."

"I promise, Mallory. I won't talk about it."

She meant it. I knew, because for once, she kept her questions quiet. I could see them burning behind her eyes, even when I left for the day.

"Come on," I told Tanya. "We're going to take care of you."

Thursday (Continued)

It was a strange thing, to feel so strong and invincible, while also so shaky and sick. Standing up to my mother was such a rush, but I had not been driving for than a minute when the exhaustion hit. My limbs felt heavy. I didn't know how I was going to get out of the car, let alone rally anyone at The Northern Grind into helping me look for Tanya.

I was determined to do such a thing, to take care of the ghost while I was still on a roll, but I came to a full stop when I saw his truck out front.

I slammed on the brakes, jolting myself forward. I was lucky, I suppose, that there was no one behind me to cause an accident. In the moment, I felt anything but blessed.

It felt like something from a nightmare. It was the same dingy blue pick-up truck, I was certain of it. I didn't know why or how he was still driving that beat up old thing after all these years, but I knew it was the same vehicle.

There was no way in hell it could be a coincidence.

A loud horn blared from behind me, which finally got me moving, and I was able to make it out safely, without being arrested for my shitty driving.

What little resolve I had to find answers about Tanya faltered. As I passed up her place of employment, and headed back home, I could feel her eyes on me.

I was ashamed, and didn't even try to explain myself.

It seemed idiotic that this inevitability hadn't dawned on me, but I truly hadn't considered that my quest for answers would put me on a collision course with him. Even if he *was* my prime suspect. Even if I was asking questions about *his* wife. I wasn't ready to see him.

I wasn't sure I would ever be ready.

There was another important step that had to be taken, though, and luckily I could take it from the comfort of my own home. When I got back to the apartment, I came clean to Eric.

Well, partially.

How do you tell your long term boyfriend that you're being haunted by your ex's wife? That you're investigating a murder only you seem to know about? That the only reason you think you know about it is because of an unspeakable thing that happened to you years ago, but have never mentioned to him?

The answer, I believe, is that you don't try to tell him all that over text.

So I didn't tell him all of it.

What I did tell him was that being back in Leyton had brought up some stuff.

Eric

What kind of stuff?

Me

Some stuff from my past. Stuff I haven't thought about in a long time.

I just had this big talk with my mom.

Serious stuff, I guess.

Eric

Do you want to talk about it?

I could call.

Me

Text is good. It's better right now.

I think I will want to talk about it.

But not yet.

Eric

I understand.

Me

Thanks.

Eric

Are you okay?

Me

No.

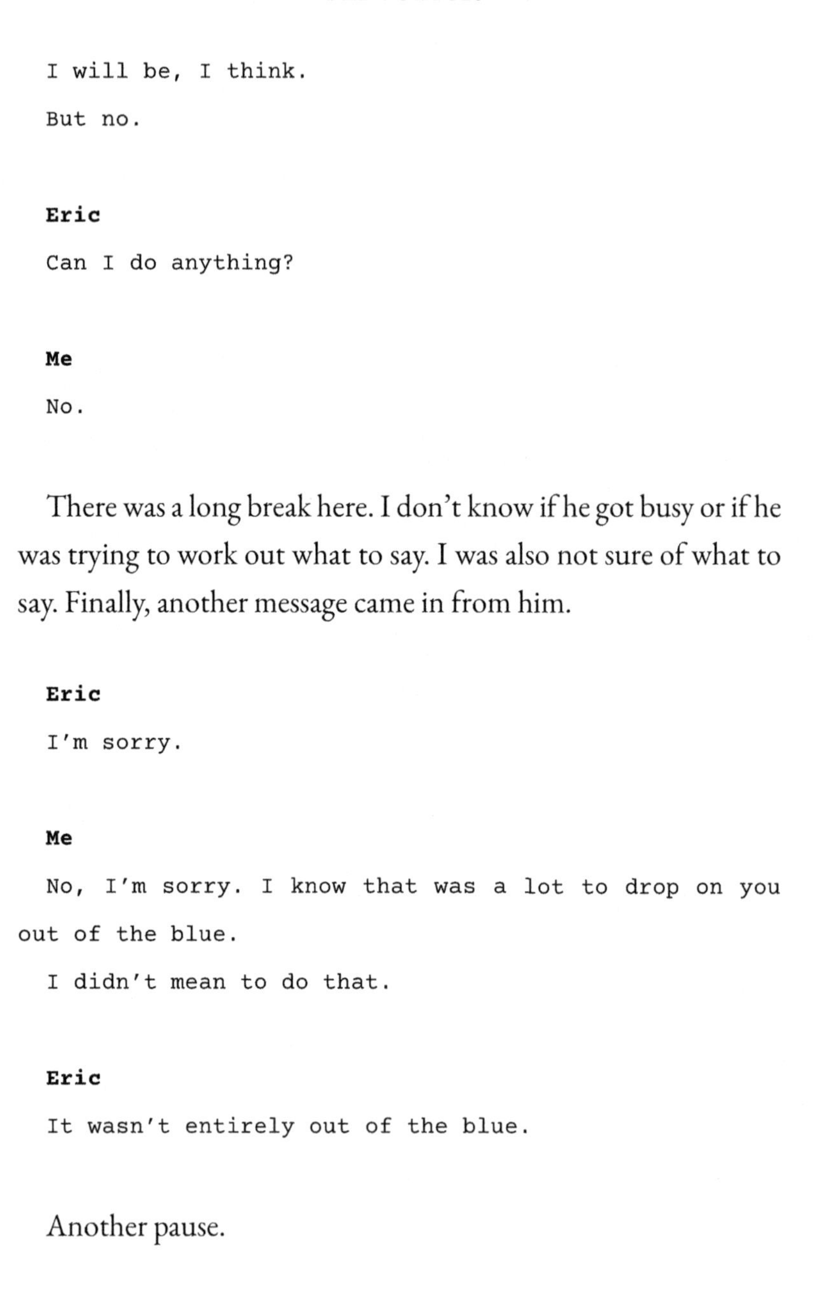

I will be, I think.

But no.

Eric

Can I do anything?

Me

No.

There was a long break here. I don't know if he got busy or if he was trying to work out what to say. I was also not sure of what to say. Finally, another message came in from him.

Eric

I'm sorry.

Me

No, I'm sorry. I know that was a lot to drop on you out of the blue.

I didn't mean to do that.

Eric

It wasn't entirely out of the blue.

Another pause.

Eric

I've been worried about you these last couple days.

I know you've been busy, but I felt like it was more than that.

Me

I'm sorry. I didn't mean to worry you.

Eric

I just want you to be okay.

Me

I know.

Eric

I wouldn't have suggested you going early if I had known.

Me

I didn't know either.

Eric

I'm glad you told me though.

I hope you know you can tell me anything.

Me

I do.

Eric

Is this why you've been sick?

Me

I think so.

I just didn't know how bad it would be.

How bad it is to be back.

Eric

I wish I was there with you.

Do you need me to come down early?

Me

No.

I wish you were here too.

But I need to work through some stuff.

Eric

I just wish I could help.

Me

I know.

But this gives me a chance to sort my shit out.

And maybe be in a better place when we talk about it face to face.

Eric

Okay.

Me

Yeah.

Eric

You'll let me know if you need anything though?

Me

I will.

Eric

Anything at all.

Me

I promise.

Eric

I love you, Mal.

Me

I love you too.

Eric

And please get some rest, okay? For me?

Me

`Yeah, heading to bed now.`

Only I didn't head to bed. This conversation, which took a couple minutes to transcribe in its entirety and hours for us to have through texts in and around our own lives, had only been the background part of my evening.

In the foreground of my Thursday night, I was working on something that even now, I'm not entirely proud of.

I was setting myself up with a VPN, and I was signing into his Facebook page, like I had promised myself I wouldn't do.

Just as I was wrapping up my communication with Eric, and about to do some snooping, I saw something that would have made it impossible for me to sleep.

Tanya Grace was online.

Thursday (Night)

Our conversation was short, but it was enough to keep me tossing and turning all night without a wink of sleep, despite my exhaustion.

There was one status update from her, posted just a minute or so before I had gotten in, saying that she'd be out of town visiting some relatives. It said she wasn't likely to be online, and her cell phone service would be spotty.

Then, she messaged me. Or the person using her account did.

Tanya

`Who is this?`

I hate to interrupt the story here, but it's obvious how I was feeling here, isn't it? Icy. Cold. Shaky. I was more afraid of whoever was posting from Tanya's account than I was afraid of Tanya, the ghost, sitting in the room with me while I read.

What I'd rather mention here, was something small I noticed in passing, and am only just unpacking now. This dialogue between the two accounts was their first set of private messages. There was no chat history between the two.

I wonder if that's just what it's like when you live with someone, but I don't think that's the case.

Eric and I, who see each other most days, all days, we still share things online across several accounts. Memes, links, videos, little love notes. I cannot imagine changing my status to married with someone, and never interacting with the account.

In the 21st century, this seems very much the portrait of an unhappy marriage. It is not as beautiful as the art of love letters, which we have lost to time, but there is a love language in our era of technology, and it was absent from this glimpse into their lives.

I digress.

I was, inspired by my personal victory from earlier, and by Tanya's ghost across from me, bold enough to answer.

Gabriel

I could ask you the same thing.

Tanya

It's me.

Is that you, Mallory?

Whatever confidence I had left me at that. I felt like he was staring at me straight through the screen.

I would have signed off, terrified, but was beaten to it.

Tanya Grace has gone offline.

Friday (Morning)

I GOT OUT OF bed when the sun rose. There was no point in setting an alarm. Even knowing I wanted to be up early, it hardly seemed like it would make a difference. I had not been sleeping a regular schedule for several days, and I didn't expect to get much deep sleep.

In the end, I got none at all.

I could well have used the rest for the long day ahead, but I was almost grateful at the time to have evaded my dreams. I didn't need to see Tanya in her lace any more than I needed to wake with bruises.

I lay in bed for a while as the pale light began to filter in through the cheap blinds of my bedroom, just looking at Tanya's face as she lay beside me.

She was so beautiful.

I don't remember ever noticing that before, how *pretty* she had been. I remember her writing, her poetry. Her unique sense of style. Those red shoes. Her precise pronunciation of awkward, German dialogue as we presented our homework. So many little things, but not her beauty.

I got lost in her eyes.

It was as close as I got to a moment of peace, but it was the kind that made me very sad. I wondered if she was still beautiful, what she might look like now, what might be left of her. I could not fathom how anyone waking up beside her in the mornings would want anything but to see her smile. I want to say that I would have given her the world. But I let her down more than almost anyone.

I could have laid there all day, looking at her, pretending I had not failed. I might have wept and apologized, and tried to make my peace with her eternal presence in my life. But I knew I had to keep trying to free her if I could, because that was the least she deserved.

Before the light grew enough to show the bruises at her neck, I was up.

I had things to do.

I started with a quick check on the tablet to make sure no new messages had come into the account. I knew—rather, felt—that it may not be the best idea to stay signed in on someone else's account after being caught, but I couldn't risk him changing his password and locking me out.

I might need access later.

When I saw nothing new, and noted Tanya was still offline, I set out.

I drove down to The Northern Grind, and was pleased to see the truck parked out in front again. It was waiting for me, but that was exactly what I wanted.

It gave me a chance to go to his house.

The way I had put it together, he had probably heard Thursday morning from my mother that I had run into Tanya, and had asked about her. Now, if he was hoping to run into me, it made a certain amount of sense that he'd be frequenting the coffee shop where he knew I'd seen her.

After confirming, I set course for the outskirts of Leyton.

There were a million things I feared may go wrong in this plan, which was filled with seemingly infinite points of failure. Maybe I couldn't find my way there. Maybe he had moved. Maybe someone else would be home. Maybe he'd get tired of looking for me and come back. Maybe a lot of things, but I was getting desperate and felt past time for a bold stroke.

The place had, mostly, gone to shit.

The house was still as squat and ugly as I remembered it. The white paint had long since ceased to be white. The yard was dried, the grass brown and shriveled, almost indistinguishable from the surrounding mud. The yard was big enough, but felt cramped and dangerous for all the rusted out vehicles that were now parked out front.

I remember the work that had been done to his truck, and wondered if he had done it himself. Someone there certainly seemed to be into cars.

It was enough to give me some hope that this was still his house, though it felt incongruent with the picture of him I had tried so hard to resist visiting in my mind. He had always been so clean, put together, taking pride in his appearance. Would this be the condition he would keep his house in? Why was there no trace of Tanya's presence there?

I parked my car in the dirt, facing the driveway in case I needed to get out in a hurry. As I walked closer to the house, I could see there was *some* trace of her after all. There were pockets of tidiness in the mess, anachronisms that had been carefully tended to, that were very much her style. There was a little herb garden just next to the steps. There was a sundial, and a half-empty bird feeder.

It was beautiful, and sad, and painful all at once to think she'd had a life here. Until she hadn't. It broke my heart to see her standing in the small garden, looking down at plants that I doubted her husband would ever water in her absence. What would happen to all the little things, when she had left them all alone?

I pushed the thoughts from my head.

There was no time.

I walked carefully through the overgrown tangles of crunchy grass, toward the back door. All the while my heart was racing. I tried to steady myself, to no avail.

My plan was half-baked at best, and I expected each and every moment for something to go wrong. I expected to be caught by someone on the property, to lie, to incriminate myself as to my true intentions somehow. If I had rolled the dice too carelessly and ended up in a confrontation with him, I didn't know what would happen. If hearing about him could send me into a fit, I didn't like to think what seeing him in the flesh would do—and that's assuming his plan hadn't been to lure me there all along.

I doubted the years has made him any wiser, or kinder. There was no telling what he'd do to me.

I wished in that moment that I owned a gun.

It was an insane, unbidden thought, that luckily proved to be needless.

I did not find him on the property, but I found *something*.

A smell.

Approaching the back of the house was like drawing near a hospital. There was the stench of bleach so strong it made my eyes water, but it was somehow not strong enough to entirely cover the undertones of fecal matter and blood.

I got as close as I thought my stomach could handle, as close as I dared. The glass of the bathroom window was broken, but the window was too high for me to get a good look. I stood on tiptoe, straining, and could only *just* see into the room. As foolish as it felt, I did my best to jump as high as I could, knowing already what was in there, but needing to see it with my own eyes.

In the end, all I got a glimpse of was black plastic.

I hadn't realized how deeply I'd been hoping to be proven wrong until that hope was shattered. I'd found what I had come looking for, but it felt like the whole world had come crashing down around me.

Friday (The Whole Day)

The one small victory broke my heart, and everything that followed was an exercise in frustration.

Worried he could be on his way back to the house, I got in my car and got the hell out of there as fast as I could. I was home, and grieving, before I realized my rather obvious mistakes in the matter.

I was expecting the trip to be another dead end, another thing to cross off my list of leads. I had not been prepared to find a body, and this was evident by the fact I had not thought to call the authorities.

I got as far as hitting 9-1 on my phone screen before I thought better of it.

It would have been one thing to tell them I was trespassing on private property, stalking my ex's wife, when I found her dead in the bathroom. It was another thing entirely to tell them not only had I been trespassing and found a body, but that I had also *fled the scene.*

I cursed myself as I set the phone back down. I decided that, this deep in shit already, it wouldn't hurt to come up with a plan as to what I would say before I made the call.

I was afraid to tell the police anything at that point.

I was beyond tired, and racked with guilt over how I had gotten to such a place in my life at all, even before the slew of terrible decisions I'd made over the past few days. I genuinely believed that if I had to report a murder, I might accidentally implicate myself in it.

Why not?

Why was Tanya haunting me if she didn't agree that I was responsible for her death as much, if not more than him?

When it comes down to it, I knew what he was, and I didn't do anything, and I hadn't been the one to pay for the price of my mistake.

That was not the sort of nuance I expected the local law enforcement to understand. It was not the sort of thing I could admit to myself in such blatant terms then, let alone try to defend to suspicious strangers.

I thought about going back.

I could make the call from there. I could say I was visiting an old friend, and I smelled something. Worried, I had gone around to the back of the house where I had found the body.

Only what if he'd gone home in the time it had taken me to find the body, drive home, and then drive back?

What if I ran into him at the coffee shop trying to see if he was there?

I was making mistakes left and right, and the trip had been a big enough risk the first time around. I knew returning was not a feasible option for me.

I decided I couldn't be involved in reporting a body, but resolved to get the police out to the property somehow.

This came in the form of a request for a wellness check, which I made promptly.

I was careful to concoct a version of the story that, while not strictly the truth, would not tangle me in any lies that could be carried to court later on. I kept it simple. I went to school with Tanya. I ran into her at the coffee shop earlier this week. She seemed off. I heard she missed work. I decided to pay her a visit to see if she needed anything, but hadn't seen her. I added that it looked like her car was in (an easy mistake with all the cars on the property) but that she had not answered the door. I was worried.

I almost brought up a history of depression, just to make the matter seem more urgent, but chose against it. My stupid, overactive writer brain had kicked back into full gear, as if making up for its previous lapses that morning, and I could see a million ways that might backfire later in a court of law. The defense lawyers could claim suicide, get charges down from pre-meditated murder down to tampering with the body. They could plead insanity, say that he was so overcome with the tragic death of his wife that he had lost control. No, I definitely didn't want any depression, real, suspected, or otherwise, entered onto the record.

It was strange to me, how the more I plotted and schemed on how to get help, the more I felt like I had been complicit in the death. And the more guilt I felt, the stronger Tanya's presence seemed to be.

It unsettled me enough that I forced myself to bite the bullet and make the call.

To my surprise, and my short-lived relief, the officers agreed immediately to the check. I didn't know if it was a slow day, or part of the city's push for better PR with the department, but my heart soared at how easy it had been. I plotted out a little scene in my head where I had timed things out perfectly, and they would catch him red-handed, trying to hide the body.

When they called me back, they told me simply that no one had been home, and they had not found anything suspicious. It was all I could do to thank them, and hope I sounded convincing. They promised me they'd keep an eye out. They assured me it was fine. I tried to keep my tone polite and normal, but the second they had hung up, I threw my phone clear across the room.

I didn't know what to make of the call.

Had they not really checked?

Were they just placating me?

Had someone beaten them to the house?

He would not have had enough time to hide the body, but he could have met them at the door with a big smile and a story about how his wife was going out of town.

I could practically see him there, at his door, giving them a toothy grin.

"Did she forget to tell her work? I'm not surprised, it's been a rough couple of days. I'll be sure to drop by and let them know."

"Who did you say called in the tip?"

"Mal? Mallory Brennan?"

"Well, how sweet of her."

"I'm just so touched to know she's thinking of us."

The scene was imaginary, but it pissed me off. It made me want to throw more things.

Instead, I pulled myself to my feet and made the first logical decision of the day. I checked the damage to my phone.

The screen was cracked badly enough that I couldn't tell if the rest was functional. There was also a dent in my wall, which didn't bode well for our security deposit.

I opened my tablet with the intention of shooting a quick email to Eric, knowing that he had alerts turned on for them and would see the pop-up immediately. I never made it that far.

There was a new message waiting for me.

Tanya

We need to talk.

I signed out of his account as quickly as I could, kicking myself for ever getting involved in this mess in the first place.

Friday (Continued)

I SENT THE EMAIL to Eric, and was almost grateful for the broken phone after that. It gave me an excuse to be a recluse. To curl up in my office chair, and cry, and give up.

Eventually though, I had to respond. Not to the private message on someone else's account, but to Tanya herself. Her expression had been questioning me for hours before I felt collected enough to say anything.

"I tried, okay?"

She just kept staring.

"God damn it, Tanya, do you not see that I tried? I went to the house. I called the police. I did what I could do."

Only she didn't budge.

"I know. I fucked up. I shouldn't have left. I should have called from there. I should have kept my eyes on those damn trash bags, and I should have made sure that the police saw what I saw but I didn't think about it, okay?"

Nothing.

"Do you want me to keep saying it? I fucked up. I'm sorry! But I was scared. I panicked, and I left, and then I didn't know how to handle it. I've never done this before. It freaked me out. Haven't you ever felt scared?"

My eyes fell to the bruises on her neck.

Look who I was talking to.

"I'm sorry, Tanya. I...should have called sooner today. I should have called years ago. I should have called in, and reported him years ago. I was just so scared. That doesn't make it right...but I can't... He scared me."

Even then, I couldn't talk about it. Broaching the topic though, it was enough to get a response from her. She didn't speak to me, but she did get up and move out of the room. She looked so real, even when she was moving. There was no blur, no translucency, nothing to indicate that she might be a ghost.

I wondered if I should have followed her, but she surprised me by coming back.

She had a glass of wine in each hand.

She offered me one.

I didn't know what to do, so I reached for it. To my surprise, my hand made contact with the stem of the glass, and I could *feel* it. I took a sip, and tasted the sweet, cloying red.

Had I bought the wine?

Had I unpacked the glasses?

I knew I had stopped at a couple stores, but I couldn't remember exactly when, or what all I had bought. It was all a blur. She was more real to me than anything else in the world just then.

She sat down on the corner of my bed and watched me, swirling her glass. She didn't drink any. I guess she didn't really have to.

There was a clear point to this encounter. She could interact with objects now. Either my ghost had reached poltergeist status, or my delusions were moving from the visual/auditory kind into something more tactile.

In either case, I didn't like what the development might mean for me.

I took another sip, and I tried to summon the courage I needed to ask my next question. "Why did you marry him?"

She looked up from her wine, and our eyes locked. She said nothing.

"You knew what he was. You were the one who tried to warn me away from him when we were dating."

I had almost forgotten that part. I couldn't place when it had come back, but now I was sure of it, that she had tried.

She had written it on the worksheet before she had passed it down to me. One simple sentence.

Er ist kein guter Mann.

She waited for me to work through it.

"You tried to warn me, and then when I left... You...you went to him anyway. Did he threaten you? Were you scared of something?"

The guilt, the wine, something twisted in my stomach as I tried to put words to my next fear.

"This whole time, were you just worried...that if it wasn't you...it would have been someone else?"

That was what *I* had been afraid of, all these years after all. Only it hadn't been an idle fear for me. It had been someone else. It had been Tanya.

She was the one person who was supposed to know better, and she had gotten shot in the crossfire.

"Only, why did you not turn him in? Why would you take it? If he hurt you, why would you let him?"

I searched her face and got only more of the same. I thought of the most hideous answer on her behalf.

"Did you *love* him?"

There was no answer, of course, but I could hardly be surprised at that notion. How often it must be, that the thing we love is the thing that kills us?

Still, it stung.

I hated the idea that he had used her, hurt her, tossed her life away, and all the while she might have loved him. I hated it so much. He hadn't deserved her love. He hadn't deserved *her*.

"Tanya, I don't know what it is you want me to do. I don't know why you're still here."

She walked over and simply poured her cup into mine. She stood over me, watching until I drank.

Deeply.

And that night, I slept.

Friday (Night)

I DON'T REALLY NEED to explain what I dreamed of, do I?

My old nightmare had come home to me to rest.

I dreamed of the night he bit me.

I dreamed about it in the same, vague way that I always did. The bits and pieces rubbing their jagged edges against each other until I woke up in a cold sweat, terrified.

I could feel the bruise re-forming on my arm where his teeth had been.

But he hadn't stopped at my arm.

And that was not the only part of me that hurt on Saturday.

Saturday (Morning)

I WAS STIFF, AND sore, but I had gotten enough rest that I had missed the dawn. I saw the two wine glasses still sitting on my desk, and wasn't sure what to make of that in regards to my sanity. I was past caring too deeply. I was more concerned with Tanya, sitting in my office chair. She stood up when she saw me looking, and gestured for me to take her place.

I did as she requested. I put my hand on the tablet and she nodded, so I opened it up. I signed into my own account, and saw the message waiting for me, as I had expected.

Gabriel

You shouldn't have involved the police.

I glanced at my ghost. Again, she nodded.

He was still online.

Mal

I know what you did.

Gabriel

Can you prove it?

Mal

Fuck you.

Gabriel

Why do you care so much?

Mal

She didn't deserve it.

There was a pause. I could see the dots of him typing bouncing up and down. I looked up to Tanya for a sign that maybe I was on the right track, that this could be my path to laying her to rest once and for all. Her eyes were off me, glued to the screen.

It seemed I had caught him off guard, and so I pressed the advantage.

Mal

She deserved better than you gave her.

She deserves to rest.

Properly.

I want to see justice done.

It felt like an eternity as I waited for the response. Finally, it came.

Gabriel

I want to see you.

Mal

Fuck you.

Gabriel

Do you want to know what happened, or not?

Mal

I know what happened.

Gabriel

I don't think you do.

But I'm willing to tell you.

Mal

Tell me then.

Gabriel

Tonight.

Do you remember the spot?

I wished I didn't remember. I wished I didn't have a clue where he meant. But I did. I could never forget that place, or what had happened there.

Mal

I do.

Gabriel

Good.

10 p.m. tonight.

Come alone.

No police.

Not if you want her to rest.

I didn't answer.

I didn't need to.

I had a feeling he'd be there, waiting for me, no matter what I did or didn't say. There was plenty of time to think it over, and I did.

I thought about it carefully, before deciding it would be a bad idea to go.

I kept thinking about it after that, too.

I thought about it while I was replacing my phone. While I made myself a sandwich. While I showered, and dressed in fresh clothes from one of the boxes. It was on the back of my mind while I called my boyfriend, and he laughed, and told me that I sounded better. That I was more relaxed. More at peace.

I realized I *was*.

At some point between denouncing the idea as idiotic and getting ready to leave, I had made peace with how things were going to end. Badly, I imagined, but I didn't care.

It didn't matter how it happened, so long as they ended.

And so I had decided to go.

Saturday 10 P.M.

I ALMOST CALLED THE police about a dozen times on the way.

Almost.

Obviously I didn't. There would be no story if I had let the professionals take care of it, and maybe I would no longer have the company of my ghost.

I was nervous, if not surprised, that she waited in the car for me as I headed into the woods.

9:30 had rolled into 9:40, then 9:50, and I was beginning to think I had gotten myself lost. The woods were dark. The path had been worn down into nothing. Everything was overgrown.

There were not even empty beer cans, or fast food wrappers, or sleeping bags, or discarded condoms. Long gone were the days of this being used as a hook up spot, I assumed, and it was dead silent.

We were alone.

The clock was ticking toward the deadline.

For as often as I had dreamed about that terrible night, I had never once stopped to recall *how* we had gotten to our spot. I had never wanted to remember, until Saturday, when 10 p.m. hit, and I was sure I had gone the wrong way.

Panic was flooding my system when I saw what I was looking for. The practically nonexistent trail turned to muddy earth up ahead. I knew without a doubt it was the right place, because I could see the depression in the ground where something heavy had been dragged along.

I followed the trail to where the two black bags sat, abandoned.

I wanted to open them, to see fully for myself, but I couldn't. I was too afraid that letting my guard down would result in me being shot or tased or otherwise incapacitated. There was only a voice from the darkness ahead.

"I didn't know if you would really come."

It took my breath away. I staggered back some as, from the tree line, emerged Tanya Grace.

She wore dark jeans, streaked with mud, and a black turtleneck sweater that was far too warm for the summer air. She had a shovel in her hand, and was looking over me, judging me as harshly as her ghost had done.

"Are the police coming?" she asked.

I shook my head.

"You're either braver than I thought, or more stupid."

I was wrong. She was not exactly as she had been in high school. It was more than just the matter of her discolored and swollen face. It was the gruff, emotionless way she spoke, the carelessness of her words. Before she had always been a deep ocean of mystery, and now every thought was right there on the surface for me to read.

She was amused.

"I feel stupid," I admitted. I didn't see the point in playing any more games. "I thought you were dead."

"I got that from our last conversation."

"You were on his account," I said pointedly.

"So were you."

I inhaled sharply. She had me there.

"Do you want to tell me why you were signing in from his page?" she asked.

"I was trying to check in on you."

"Why?"

How could I even try to explain what I had been going through? "I saw you at the coffee shop. The ring. The bruises. I...wanted to talk to you. To see if you were okay. And then when you didn't show up..."

"You thought he killed me?"

"Maybe."

"You thought he killed me because *you* came back?"

I looked over the bruises and cuts on her face. "I didn't know what to think. I was just trying to find out."

"Not everything is about you, Mal."

What could I tell her then, but the truth? "You were haunting me."

She regarded me carefully. "I can take care of myself."

"Clearly."

She looked almost insulted as she brushed two, gloved fingers across her cheek. "This is nothing."

"It doesn't look like nothing."

"I gave it to him worse."

My eyes fell back to the two trash bags at her feet. It took a long time for her meaning to sink in. Longer than it should have.

"You killed him?"

"I didn't ask you out here to bury lawn clippings."

"My mom saw him. At the store. Twice. She saw him Thursday."

I was struggling with the timeline, trying to piece together what had really happened outside of the story I'd been telling myself.

"It must have been in the morning, if she did."

"But his truck..."

"*My* truck. He gave it to me."

I had to think back to when exactly I had seen it, how careful I had been to keep my distance. "I thought he was waiting to run into me," I explained.

"You were half right. I went in to get my last paycheck, and Robbie told me there was a girl in asking questions about me. Poking around. Acting weird. I was going to tell you to knock it the hell off."

I didn't know what to say.

The story checked out.

Even if it hadn't, there was more than enough evidence in front of me to put aside my own narrative of events.

"I just can't believe he's dead."

"Are you sorry?"

"No," I said. "I'm not."

Indeed, it felt like a great weight had been lifted from my shoulders. Something loosened in my chest. I could breathe easier.

"Are you going to turn me in?"

"No." I was surprised, again, at how little I had to think about the answer.

"Then here,"—she handed me the shovel—"let's finish this together."

I took it, and she showed me where the grave was.

We were knee deep in the brambles, which she had pushed away from an area just wide enough to dig. We took turns holding the flashlight and pulling back the thorny foliage, while the other dug deep.

One of the bags burst open when I kicked it into the hole. Blood and shit—and whatever other fluids—splashed up onto my jeans.

I emptied my stomach again, but then we kept going.

The whole thing felt like a dream, like I was watching someone else do it. I may as well have been a witness to two strangers burying my nightmares for me.

It was cathartic, and strangely, it was as calm as I had felt all week despite the madness of it all. My mind was so clear that I was almost surprised to hear my voice.

"I just have one question."

"Sure."

"Why were you with him?"

"Why were you?"

It came crashing back to me then, what my mother had said about him. How she had never seen a boy so much in love. How he had spoiled me. The manner in which he presented himself. He never showed up to my house without a gift, and sweet nothings to whisper in my ear. He had cradled my head against his chest when my dad had died. We had looked like the perfect couple from the outside, and the illusion had been so pretty I had never dared break it for anyone but myself.

So in that moment, I understood.

His relationships had been selfish, and corroded, but the feelings were not born from nothing. They were cultivated. And they looked so real.

I was glad, overwhelmingly so, that the romantic side of him had died with the rest.

When all was said and done, there was a faint smell in the grass I knew for certain would wash away, and some overturned dirt beneath brambles that no one would ever check. Any evidence that something terrible had happened here was buried deep.

The world had been restored to its natural order. I believed that so strongly that I almost couldn't fathom finding my ghost still in the car, waiting for me.

Epilogue

AND HERE WE ARE.

I'm sure, my dear hypothetical reader, that you have made it to the end with a few questions of your own.

After all, you thought this was a ghost story.

Perhaps you are like me in that regard. Maybe you even thought that once I knew Tanya was alive and well and had come out on top, the guilt would vanish, and my ghost would be gone.

Yet here she is, still watching me.

I hate to tell you, but things are never so easy.

Two nights and a day have come and gone and I have put my story to paper, just the way I experienced it, just the way it happened. A second day is slipping through my fingers, but I am finally, finally at the end.

I hope.

It is nice to think that this will be the act where my ghost, this memory of Tanya, this longing for a better life we never got, can be laid to rest. I want to believe I'll wake alone in the bed tomorrow, having not dreamed. The truth is that I don't know what my apologies are really worth in the face of all my regrets.

I have carried them for a long time, and now, by reading this, you will carry a piece of them as well.

If it helps you bear the burden, I can tell you the one thing that I have learned.

Sometimes it's the living who haunt us the most.

Acknowledgements

A big thank you to everyone who went on this strange ride with me. Tasha, in particular, who read an early draft and helped me get it ready for submission. Ruth Anna has also been a vocal supporter that I should pursue my saddest stories, and here we are.

I have so much gratitude as well for the team at Slashic Horror Press. David-Jack had to work with me and my nonsense on The Desert Island Game, and then still somehow decided that it was worth doing it all again to bring you this. Lee has been incredible both times around. The other Slashic authors have started to feel like my family, and I am just so lucky to be in the rotation a second time.

I have to thank Christy for being such a joy to work with and providing the cover. She did the art for my debut book last year, and I was so excited when I was asked about getting to work with her again. She is one of the kindest and most talented people working in the indie horror space today.

Last, but certainly not least, thank you to *you*. Reading this. Yes, you. I wouldn't get to do what I loved if it weren't for readers dedicated to reading the smaller voices in strange, queer fiction. Your support means everything to me.

About the Author

Cat Voleur is an author of strange horror fiction, and a proud mother to all the rescued felines. You can find her co-hosting Slasher Radio and The Nic F'n Woo Cage Cast. When she's not creating or consuming morbid content you can find her pursuing her passion for fictional languages.

Website: catvoleur.com

Twitter: @Cat_Voleur

Printed in Great Britain
by Amazon